Copyright © 2021 by Miranda Harmon
All Rights Reserved
HOLIDAY HOUSE is registered in the U.S. Patent and Trademark Office.
Printed and bound in December 2020 at Leo Paper, Heshan, China.
The artwork was created digitally.
www.holidayhouse.com
First Edition
1 3 5 7 9 10 8 6 4 2

Library of Congress Cataloging-in-Publication Data

Names: Harmon, Miranda, author, illustrator.
Title: Spring cakes / Miranda Harmon.
Description: First edition. | New York : Holiday House, 2021. | Series:
I like to read comics | Audience: Ages 4–8. | Audience: Grades K–1.
Summary: "Three kittens, Nutmeg, Cinnamon, and Ginger, go on a quest to
find the magical ingredients to make Mama Cat's famous cupcakes"—
Provided by publisher.
Identifiers: LCCN 2020031470 | ISBN 9780823447534 (hardcover)
Subjects: CYAC: Graphic novels. | Brothers and sisters—Fiction.
Cats—Fiction. | Animals—Infancy—Fiction. | Baking—Fiction.
Magic—Fiction.
Classification: LCC PZ7.7.H3657 Spr 2021 | DDC 741.5/973—dc23
LC record available at https://lccn.loc.gov/2020031470

ISBN: 978-0-8234-4753-4 (Hardcover)

Cakes

Miranda Harmon

HOLIDAY HOUSE · NEW YORK

This year we are old enough to help!

Good morning, kittens!

Today we will make spring cakes.

The cakes are magic. I need you to get special ingredients.

After you get everything on this list, we will make the cakes.

- flour
- honey
- eggs
- berries
- roses

The kittens quickly eat their porridge.

First we will need flour from the old mill.

Then silver honey from the beekeeper.

Blue eggs from the chicken farmer.

Wild strawberries that grow in only one spot in the meadow.

And magical roses from the witch's garden.

Well, if it isn't the kittens! Is your mom making spring cakes?

Yes. This year we're helping!

We need some silver honey, please.

This honey is special. It is a nice spring treat.

The bees use pollen from magical flowers. The flowers only bloom in winter.

The kittens walk through the woods.

SNAP!

HOOT HOOT

A shadow crosses their path!

Save me a spring cake.

Goodbye!

The kittens walk home.

First we mix the dry ingredients.

Cinnamon measures the flour. Nutmeg measures the baking powder.

Ginger measures out spices and puts them in.

Mom puts in the sugar.

Can I break the eggs yet?

No, not yet, Ginger!

The kittens work on their own cupcakes.

Each one is special.

Just like them!

Look at our cakes!

What pretty cakes. I'm so proud!

Now it is spring, and the kittens have a picnic.